Alison's Puppy

Marion Dane Bauer

Laurie Spencer

Hyperion Books for Children
New York

For Terry, daughter of my heart
—M. D. B.

Text © 1997 by Marion Dane Bauer.
Illustrations © 1997 by Laurie Spencer.

Printed in the United States of America.

5 7 9 10 8 6

The artwork for each picture is prepared using pencil.

The book is set in 20-point Berkeley Book.

Library of Congress Cataloging-in-Publication Data

Bauer, Marion Dane.
Alison's puppy / by Marion Dane Bauer. — 1st ed.
p.   cm.
Summary: All Alison wants is a puppy for her birthday.
ISBN 0-7868-1140-4 (pbk.) — ISBN 0-7868-2237-6 (lib. bdg.)
[1. Dogs—Fiction. 2. Birthdays—Fiction.] I. Title.
PZ7.B3262Aj   1997
[Fic]—dc20   96-7464

Contents

Alison's birthday was coming.

"I want a puppy," she told everyone. "More than anything in the world."

"More than a doll with dancing shoes?" asked her mother.

Alison nodded. "More than a doll with dancing shoes."

"More than your own baseball bat?" asked her father.

1

Alison nodded again. "More than my own baseball bat."

"More than a new video game?" asked her big brother, Mike.

Alison nodded yet again. "More than a new video game."

"Even more than in-line skates?" asked Cindy, Alison's best friend.

Alison thought for a long time. Then she nodded. Hard. "Even more than in-line skates.

"A puppy," she said, "would play with me when I'm happy. A puppy would lick me when I'm sad. A puppy would sleep close beside me. I'd never be scared."

"A puppy would always need you," her grandpa said. "Puppies are nice."

But Alison's mother said, "No puppies. They bark."

Alison's father said, "No puppies. They dig holes in the yard."

"Puppies piddle," Mike said. "Everywhere!"

Still, Alison wanted a puppy.

More than anything in the world.

•2•

"My birthday is coming," Alison said. "And I want a puppy. More than anything in the world."

So she carried a rope to school. "Just in case," she explained to Cindy. "In case I meet a puppy who wants to come home with me."

"Good idea," Cindy said.

But when they met a Saint Bernard, Cindy hid behind a tree.

The Saint Bernard was enormous. His mouth was

huge. He licked Alison's face.
Even his tongue was large.

"*Mmmmblmfff,*" Alison said.
"My birthday is coming. Do you
want to come home with me?"
She held out the rope.

The Saint Bernard drooled on the rope. Then he drooled on Alison's shoes. Both of them at once.

Far away, someone whistled. The Saint Bernard bounded off. Cindy came out from behind the tree. "That dog was much too big," she said.

"And too wet," Alison agreed.

She wiped her face with her sleeve. She wiped her shoes on the grass. Then she wiped the rope.

At school she put the rope in her desk. "We'll go home the long way," she told Cindy.

"Why?" Cindy asked.

"So we can meet more dogs."

"I think I have to go home the short way," Cindy replied. "My mother said."

•3•

Alison walked home from school the long way. Alone.

Down the block. Through the alley. Behind the church. Across Elm Street. Past the pink house. Over the bridge in the park and along the tall iron fence.

She met lots of dogs.

She met a German shepherd on

the end of a leash. His owner was on the other end.

The shepherd smiled. He had a million teeth. His owner smiled, too, and pulled hard on the leash.

Alison met a poodle. The poodle's toes were painted red. She had a red bow on her head and a snooty expression.

Alison met a basset hound who looked tired.

A bulldog looked cross.

A tiny Mexican hairless looked cold.

And then, at last, Alison met a
puppy. The puppy didn't look
like anything at all. Just a puppy.

All floppy ears and flapping
tail. And wiggles.

The puppy wiggled under a
fence. He wiggled
across the sidewalk.
Then he rolled onto
his back. And
wiggled some
more.

"Do you bark?" Alison asked. "Do you dig holes in the yard?"

The puppy wiggled harder. His tail wiggled, too.

Alison tied the rope to the puppy's collar. "I bet you don't even piddle," she said. "Mom and Dad and Mike will love you."

The puppy wiggled on the end of the rope. All the way home.

•4•

"My birthday is coming," Alison
reminded her mother. "He would
play with me when I'm happy,"
she said, patting the puppy's head.

"No," Mom said. "Puppies chew."

"My birthday is coming," Alison
said to her father. She scratched
the puppy behind one ear. "He
would lick me when I'm sad."

"Absolutely not," Dad replied. "Puppies drag in dirt."

"A puppy would sleep close beside me," Alison said to Mike. "I'd never be scared."

Mike said nothing. He was too busy playing with the puppy.

"I want a puppy more than *anything*," Alison cried.

Dad looked tired. Mom looked sad.

"Dad and I go to work," Mom said. "You and Mike go to school. What would the puppy do?"

"He would wait for me," Alison said. But Dad shook his head. "He would chew," Dad said. "He would dig holes in the yard. He would make messes."

"Not my puppy," Alison told them.

"Puppies are puppies," Dad told her. "And besides. This puppy does not belong to you."

Grandpa patted the puppy's

head. He scratched him behind one ear. "I'll help you take him back," he said to Alison.

So Alison and Grandpa and the puppy walked back the long way. Very slowly.

Alison showed Grandpa the fence and she showed Grandpa the hole.

The puppy sniffed the fence. He sniffed the hole. Then he wiggled back into his yard.

"Ferdinand," a woman cried. "My baby!"

Alison looked at Grandpa. Grandpa looked at Alison.

"I have a rope," Alison told the woman. "You can tie your puppy. Just until the hole is fixed."

"Thank you very much," the woman said.

Alison and Grandpa walked home. Grandpa held her hand the whole way.

Still, Alison wanted a puppy.

More than anything in the world.

•5•

Alison went to the library. "My birthday is coming," she told the librarian. "I want books about dogs. Books I can read myself. Lots of them."

So the librarian looked and looked. She found eight books for Alison. *Harry, the Dirty Dog*.

Clifford, the Big Red Dog. And six
Henry and Mudge books.

Alison read and read.

Harry hated baths. Clifford ran
after lions. He dug up trees. He
caught cars.

Mudge was just about perfect.

He played with Henry. He
licked Henry. He even slept
beside Henry at night.

But he wasn't a puppy. He was
a grown dog. A big one, too.

And he already belonged to
Henry.

Besides, Mudge lived in a book.

Alison patted the air beside her chair. Just where Mudge's head would be. If she had a Mudge.

"It's all right," she said to the imaginary Mudge. "You don't need to lick me. I'm not so very sad."

But she was.

·6·

Alison's birthday arrived.

She got a doll with dancing shoes. From Mom.

She got her own baseball bat. From Dad.

A new video game. From Mike.

And Cindy drew her a picture of a puppy wearing in-line skates. And she gave her a pretty blue

bow for her hair.

Grandpa hugged her.

Alison's birthday was over and she went to bed. She went to bed,

and she lay very still.

Grandpa knocked on her door. "Are you awake?" he asked. "You didn't open my present yet."

He was holding a big box. He set it on Alison's bed.

Inside the box, something moved.

Alison looked at the box. She

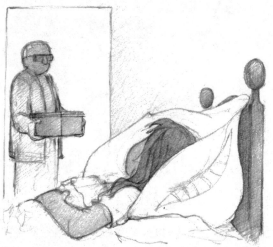

looked at Grandpa.

"Puppies bark," she reminded him. "Puppies piddle and chew. Puppies dig holes in the yard. They drag in dirt. They make messes."

"I know," Grandpa said.

Alison touched the box. She wanted to open it. She didn't want to open it.

"Shall I help?" Grandpa asked.

"Please," Alison said.

So Alison held her breath while Grandpa lifted the lid.

Slowly, slowly, Alison leaned over. Carefully, she peeked inside. And from deep, dark inside the box a tiny voice said . . .

"Meow!"

·7·

Alison lay curled in her bed. Alone. Well, almost alone.

"My birthday is over," she said to the ginger kitten.

The kitten washed his paw.

"And I wanted a puppy."

The kitten washed his other paw.

"More than anything in the world."

The kitten washed his face.

"A puppy would play with me when I'm happy."

The kitten washed his whiskers.

"A puppy would lick me when I'm sad."

The kitten washed his tail.

"A puppy would sleep close beside me." Alison closed her

eyes. "So I would never be scared."

The kitten stepped on Alison's stomach. He walked across her chest and he curled up on her pillow. Right next to her ear.

Then he touched her cheek with his cool nose. And he said, *"Mew?"*

It sounded very much like "Please?"

Alison stroked the soft fur. She whispered, "A puppy would always need me."

The kitten rumbled into a purr.

·8·

Alison gave her kitten kibble. She put fresh water in his bowl. She found him a striped ball to play with.

And she cleaned the litter box.
Mike just held his nose.

Then Alison made a soft nest in
front of the living-room window.
Her kitten would be the first to
see her when she came home
from school.

"What a nice kitten!" Mom said. "He is so quiet."

"What a nice kitten!" Dad said. "He is so clean."

"What a nice kitten!" Mike giggled. "He piddles in a box."

"Yes," Alison agreed. "He is a very nice kitten."

Dad said, "Shall we name him Puff?"

Mom asked, "What about Fluffy?"

"I know!" Mike cried. "Let's call him Tiger."

But Alison shook her head. "I already named him," she said. "A long time ago."

Mom and Dad and Mike looked at one another. Then they looked

at Alison. They were waiting.

Alison laughed. She picked up her kitten. She gave him a big hug.

"Didn't you know?" she said. "His name is Puppy!"

And Puppy purred.

Puzzling Puppy Puzzles

Doggone it! We're sure these puzzles will tickle your funny bone.

The Dog Search

Alison wanted a puppy so badly for her birthday. She would have settled for any type of dog. In this word search, the name of seven types or breeds of dogs are hidden. The words go up, down, sideways, backward, and diagonally.

Look for:														
	L	S	M	Y	B	A	C	E	L	S	H	U	R	B	X
BULLDOG	O	P	S	T	D	G	O	O	S	O	R	T	X	U	G
POODLE	C	O	C	K	E	R	S	P	A	N	I	E	L	L	O
BEAGLE	O	O	X	L	L	O	Z	X	Z	Y	Z	W	X	L	D
COCKER SPANIEL	O	D	U	D	G	G	N	A	M	R	E	B	O	D	P
SHEEPDOG	X	L	V	Q	A	G	R	Z	R	T	X	W	X	O	E
DOBERMAN	B	E	M	P	E	G	U	V	E	L	P	M	Z	G	E
ST. BERNARD	B	H	S	T	B	E	R	N	A	R	D	E	N	B	H
	X	U	V	W	M	N	O	X	P	Z	Z	A	C	B	S

The Joke's on You

What do you get when you cross a puppy with a clock? To find the answer to this riddle, cross out all the boxes above the equations that do not equal ten. Write the remaining letters on the spaces below.

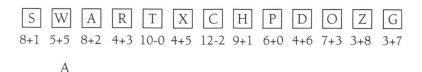

S	W	A	R	T	X	C	H	P	D	O	Z	G
8+1	5+5	8+2	4+3	10-0	4+5	12-2	9+1	6+0	4+6	7+3	3+8	3+7

A __ __ __ __ __ __ __ __

A Not-So-Perfect Party

Alison got lots of great gifts at her birthday party, but not the one she really wanted. But Alison's birthday party isn't the only one that went wrong. In the party scene below, there are ten things that are wrong. Find and circle all ten things.

All Tied Up!

These dogs' leashes got all tangled up. To find out which dog belongs to the little girl, follow the squiggly lines.

What's in a Name?

Alison named her fluffy-haired kitten Puppy. If you look closely at this picture, you'll see that there's more to it than meets the eye. The word PUPPY is hidden in the scene several times. How many times can you find the word PUPPY?

Puzzle Answers
The Dog Search

```
L  S  M  Y  B  A  C  E  L  S  H  U  R (B) X
O (P) S  T  D  G  O  O  S  O  R  T  X (U)(G)
(C  O  C  K (E) R  S  P  A  N  I  E  L) L  O
O (O) X  L (L) O  Z  X  Z  Y  Z  W  X  L  D
O (D) U  D (G) G (N  A  M  R  E  B  O (D) P
X (L) V  Q (A) G  R  Z  R  T  X  W  X (O) E
B (E) M  P (E) G  U  V  E  L  P  M  Z (G) E
B  H (S  T (B) E  R  N  A  R  D) E  N  B  H
X  U  V  W  M  N  O  X  P  Z  Z  A  C  B (S)
```

The Joke's On You
A WATCH DOG

All Tied Up!
Dog #3

A Not So Perfect Party

What's in a Name?